Outside the Window

Outside the Window

by **ANNA EGAN SMUCKER**

illustrated by **STACEY SCHUETT**

QUARRIER PRESS • Charleston, West Virginia

Quarrier Press
Charleston, WV 25302

Previously published by Alfred A Knopf, Inc.

Library of Congress Cataloging-in-Publication Data
Smucker, Anna Egan.
Outside the window / by Anna Egan Smucker ; illustrated by Stacey Schuett.
 p.   cm.
Summary: A mother bird describes the bedtime activities of a little boy to her five curious babies.
ISBN 1-891852-40-x

[1. Bedtime—Fiction.   2. Birds—Fiction.]   I. Schuett, Stacey, ill.   II. Title.
PZ7.S66478Ou 1994
[E]—dc20   92-33452

Published in the United States by Quarrier Press

Printed in Hong Kong

    10 9 8 7 6 5 4 3 2 1

Distributed by
West Virginia Book Company
1125 Central Ave.
Charleston, WV 25302
www.wvbookco.com

For Kara, Emily, and Stephanie
—A.E.S.

For Erika Kay, with love
—S.S.

On *a strong leafy branch* outside the bedroom
window of a little boy, there is a nest. In that nest live a
mother bird and her five baby birds. The biggest one
loves to eat. The medium-sized one loves to play. The
cleanest one loves to take baths. The chirpiest one loves
to hear stories. And the tiniest one is always sleepy. But
they are all very curious about the little boy who lives in
the house that their nest in the maple tree can almost touch.

In the evening, when the air cools and the sky turns
pink, Mother Bird tucks her babies safely down into their
nest. The nest sways gently back and forth in the green-
leaved maple tree. And every evening, from the darkness
of the nest, the baby birds ask their mother questions
about what the little boy is doing.

"Is he asleep yet?" asks the little bird who is always sleepy— and who is almost asleep already.

"No, not yet," says Mother Bird. "He is still playing outside."

"Playing?...Still?" asks the little bird who loves to play. "What is he playing?"

"He is making sand pies in his sandbox," says Mother Bird.

"Sand pies? Does the boy eat the sand pies?" asks the little bird who is always hungry.

"No, little one," says Mother Bird. "He doesn't eat the sand pies. He likes juicier things than that."

"Yum," says the hungry little bird. And he imagines the little boy eating a juicy bedtime snack.

"Do I hear water running?" asks the little bird who loves to bathe.

"Yes," says Mother Bird. "The boy is taking his bath."

"Ooh," says the little bird, shivering under his downy feathers. And he imagines the little boy splashing in cool water.

"Is he asleep yet?" asks the sleepy little bird, very sleepily.

"No, not yet," says Mother Bird. "He is brushing his teeth."

"What are 'teeth'?" ask the other baby birds.

"They are big white things inside his beak." says Mother Bird.

"Oh," the baby birds say, wishing they had teeth in their beaks.

"Is he asleep yet?" asks the sleepy little bird, with his eyes closed.

"No, not yet," says Mother Bird. "But he is climbing into his bed now."

"*Mmm,*" says the sleepy little bird, imagining the boy snuggling down in his nest.

"Is it time for the story?" asks the little bird who loves stories.

"Yes, it is time for the story," says Mother Bird. "The boy's mother is opening the book."

"What is the story about?" asks the little bird who loves stories.

"It's about a mother bird and her baby birds," says Mother Bird.

"Oh," says the little bird, and imagines a story all about herself.

"Is the boy asleep yet?" asks the sleepy little bird, in a voice so soft his mother can hardly hear it.

"No, not yet," says Mother Bird. "He is saying his prayers."

"How does he say his prayers?" ask the other baby birds.

"He looks out the window at us and at the stars," says Mother Bird.

"Oh," the little birds say, feeling very important and lifting their heads to try to see the stars too.

"Is the boy asleep . . . yet?" asks the sleepy little bird,
too tired to raise his head.

"Almost," says Mother Bird. "His mother is tucking
him in and kissing him good night."

"*Mmm,*" the little birds say, snuggling closer together in
their dark, warm nest.

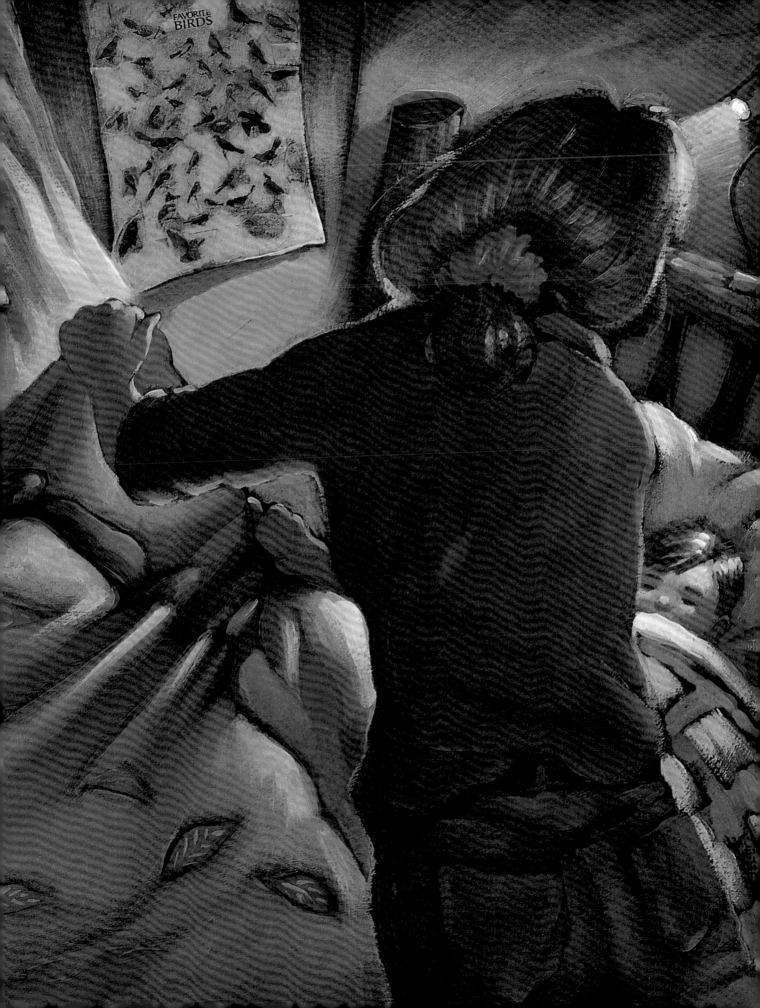

"Is . . . the boy . . . asleep . . . yet?" ask all the little birds, yawning.

"Yes, the boy is asleep now," says Mother Bird.

"Ah," the little birds say and close their sleepy eyes.

"Good night, sweet dreams," says Mother Bird. And she spreads her soft wings over the baby birds and over the round bowl of their nest that rocks in the strong arms of the maple tree—outside the window of the sleeping boy .

ANNA EGAN SMUCKER is the author of *No Star Nights*, winner of the 1990 International Reading Association Children's Book Award in the Younger Reader category. Her other books include *A History of West Virginia*, and *To Keep the South Manitou Light* — a historical fiction novel for young readers. With her husband, Kim, she has written parts of more than thirty workbooks and student texts in the areas of reading and social studies, and has worked as a teacher, librarian, and writer-in-residence. In addition to writing, Anna Egan Smucker gives author presentations and conducts writing workshops throughout the country. She makes her home in Bridgeport, West Virginia.

STACEY SCHUETT has illustrated many critically praised books for children, including *Alex and the Wednesday Chess Club* by Janet Wong, *Pleasing the Ghost* by Sharon Creech and her own *Somewhere In the World Right Now*. She lives in Northern California with her family, where she watches birds come and go in the trees around her studio.